Tennessee's Ghostly Legends

By

Tammy J. Poore

Illustrated by

Tammy J. Poore

Nine Lives Publishing

Knoxville, TN 37918

Dedicated to those of like mind,

And Similar tastes.

Those of us who can't resist a chilling tale.

Especially tales from our own hometown, region or state.

Contents:

Acknowledgements:

I owe many thanks to my very supportive family members. Each one listening to my ideas and fascinations. This book, however, couldn't have happened without my friends. Five people who joined me on ghostly adventures, or told me about a "haunted place" or researched some "haunted areas" with me.

You know who *you* are, and *I thank you!!*

Tennessee's Ghostly Legends

Preface:

I have put together a simple book of ten original ghost tales, all originating from localities in East Tennessee, near my hometown in Anderson County where I grew up, and surrounding Knox County where I currently reside.

If you are from this area, I hope you recognize some of the locations. I had to change some of the names of the characters and/or businesses to protect the establishments and to protect the living. The *dead*, however, continue to haunt us, in hopes we will recognize their identities, their story, or their tragedy.

If you are from other regions, states, or countries, I hope you will discover the many haunted places around you. There is nothing better than driving by a reputed haunted house, *or living in one!* Or dining in an eatery where the spirits of previous owners or employees check in on a regular basis. How about watching a scary movie in an actual haunted theater??? Those type of haunted places are right here in this book. ENJOY!!

Chapter 1

A Ghostly Concession Surprise
(Oak Ridge, TN)

Some of the best discoveries happen accidentally. Let me share a brief explanation of *how* I made the discovery of the haunted theater which is our primary subject. Finding out about the theater was to get 3 ghost stories in one. What a pleasantry!

While I was writing as a monthly contributor for an online newspaper I was researching the claim of several 'ghostly encounters' at a notable restaurant located in The Jackson Square Plaza. Much to my disappointment the owners of the restaurant would NOT allow me to investigate their establishment. The female owner hinted that she knew of the ghost, she informed me that the male owner did not want to discuss it.

Even though I revealed that I had interviewed several individuals who had seen the spirit of the deceased previous owner while visiting the restaurant, (hint, it was NOT a restaurant when he owned it.) Out of respect for the current owners I will not identify the restaurant, or name the previous owner, or the type of business it formerly was.

Yet that encounter led up to discovering 2 more haunted locations in Oak Ridge. While speaking to the female owner of the restaurant one of her employees overheard us discussing the 'haunting', and later contacted me to tell me about another 'haunted business' also located in Jackson Square. It's an interesting tale to say the least. Both of the people she told me to contact claimed they *had* witnessed 'probable ghostly activity' at this business. One of those people was the current business owner, who I deem to be a reliable source. This lady believed there was a spirit there and the creepy 'activity' spawned her to share a video via the internet showing an unexplained movement in a back room. Security cameras noted movement and triggered the recording, which revealed an unidentifiable *'form'* in motion, *'floating'* from behind a shelf, across the floor and *'through'* the closed and locked glass door. The figure was floating above the floor and measured at least 4 feet in height, yet it wasn't solid enough to describe accurately, it seemed to be a *'vapor'*, dull gray in color. As a result of that research, the owner of the store who shared the video online told me that she knew two unrelated individuals who had previously worked at a theater, which had been in the Grove Center shopping center, which was reputed to be haunted as well, insisting the story would be more fitting to the kind of material I collect for my books. It turns out, she would be correct.

The establishment, our subject for this chapter, was built circa 1942-1944; it was once a performance hall, later converted into a three-screen cinema after the war. It has had many face lifts over the years. For more than half a dozen years it sat vacant until it was recognized for the gem in the rough that it is and was purchased for a higher purpose, so to speak. (Another hint, my friends.)

The specific ghostly encounter I found most interesting reaches back to the mid 1970's, a time period when I can recall watching movies at *this exact theater* when I was a child. (The most memorable movie I saw at this location was titled "Freaky Friday", which was released in 1976. To think that I had been inside the theater countless times, an unsuspecting, youthful audience member and I could have possibly "sensed" a ghostly presence had I been more aware, but for all intense purposes the movies captured my attention instead.)

The mature gentleman who spoke with me actually had a ghostly encounter back in the 1970's. He experienced an unexplainable happening while working there when he was a senior at Oak Ridge High School, employed part time at the theater. Jim enjoyed his job, telling me "It was a great place to work. I got discounts for close family members to see movies. It was a luxury in my youth to go to a theater to watch a movie." Jim's job entailed whatever was needed from running concessions to cleaning the auditoriums. He had closed the theater many times before and had never seen or heard anything out of the ordinary. On this night, however, that all changed.

"There were only three of us working that night, we were shorthanded from the onset, and soon after the theater closed it was just me and one other person, Emily." Jim recounted, "I'm not sure what was special about that night, if it was a full moon or near Halloween, but I remember that it was one of those evenings when nothing went right. We had trouble in theater two, the projector stopped advancing the film and Bill had to fix the problem, I went in there once when a customer complained and we had to rethread the film, but it happened more than twice that night." Jim also recalls having trouble with the popcorn machine, the bulb that keeps the popped popcorn warm repeatedly went out, and "Whenever I attempted to replace the bulb it would light up again as soon as I touched it. I tightened the bulb and it worked fine for a few minutes, but then it would go out again. I know it went out at least five times that night." He recounted.

After the theater closed he and Emily busily cleaned the lobby. The concession stand had closed an hour prior to the last film ending, soon after the ticket box had closed. After the last patron was out they locked the doors and all three employees worked diligently to get the theater ready for the next day, Bill left before they did. Jim said, "I made sure the doors were locked after Bill left."

Jim had swept the area around the concession stand earlier and was finishing his duties in the front lobby. Emily was running a vacuum cleaner on the carpeted areas. Jim kept finding pieces of popcorn on the floor. "I would find a few pieces of popcorn in places where I had already swept." He claims, "I can assure you I was a hard worker and I wouldn't have left food on the floor."

Finally, after he re-swept the same area three times he started to think Emily was playing a practical joke. Or that Bill had snuck back in, with the help of his accomplice coworker, of course.

"I looked and saw Emily pushing the vacuum cleaner, I had heard it making noise the whole time, but to be sure it wasn't Emily playing a prank, I checked on her with my own eyes and she was engrossed in performing her duties. I was convinced someone was playing a practical joke. I searched the bathrooms, movie auditoriums and there was no one anywhere so I checked the exterior doors, they were all locked. Emily saw me prowling around and turned off the vacuum cleaner. She approached me." Jim recalls, "She asked me why I was acting nervous?"

He didn't realize he had been acting nervous, he had made an attempt to find out who was tossing popcorn on the floor, but he wasn't acting nervous. "I asked Emily what she meant."

Emily looked at him and said, "You're up to something. You're throwing popcorn on the floor, making me vacuum over spots I've already done. I would like to go home sometime tonight." The tone of her voice verified her alienation with him.

Jim assured her that he had nothing to do with it. "The same thing has been happening to me, that's why I was looking in every room and checking doors, I thought Bill had let himself back in to play a joke on us."

Jim said it was then that he started to feel worried. But a ghost was the last thing on his mind; he was more concerned that there might be an intruder.

He and Emily began a thorough search, covering every inch of the theater and found no one present. "That's when I started to feel chilled as the thought of something inhuman popped into my mind. I didn't mention it to Emily, there was no reason to, but I decided it would be a good idea to leave. So I told Emily we could go, the place looked good enough." But it didn't, Jim says he looked and there were more popcorn kernels on the floor. He bent down to pick the stray pieces up and when he raised up he saw a movement behind the concessions counter. He rushed around the counter hoping to catch sight of whoever, or whatever, it was, feeling perplexed when there was no one there.

Emily asked Jim, "What are you doing?"

Jim wouldn't admit he had seen a shadowy movement, so he told her he was double checking things. He pulled the keys out of his pocket and said, "Let's go. This night has been a long enough." He and Emily exited the building, as he turned to lock the door he thought he saw another shadowy movement. Jim hesitated, at that moment he was thinking about dismissing what he had just seen. But he couldn't do that, it didn't feel right. If someone was inside the building he couldn't lock them in and leave them all night.

"We always left a light on," Jim explained, "Although it was dark outside, the inside of the theater was dimly lit and I know I saw a full sized shadow move away from the lobby. So I told Emily to stand at the door while I looked one more time inside." Jim went back in and searched the theater a final time. "I was completely alone in that building. But by this time the hairs on the back of my neck were standing up. I didn't believe in ghosts until that night,"

This wouldn't be Jim's only encounter with the ghost but it was his first. After that night he admits he was more alert to peculiar happenings. It seemed odd noises and unexplainable equipment malfunctions were happening more often. A few weeks later he was closing again, this time he was operating the vacuum cleaner and a gal named Audrey was cleaning the restroom.

Jim explained, "I could smell fresh popcorn. That isn't unusual in a theater but we had emptied the popcorn machine nearly two hours earlier. This smelled like freshly made popcorn. The familiar smell wafted right up to me so I turned off the vacuum cleaner and walked over to the concession stand. The popcorn machine was empty, silent and dark and the smell was no longer viable." Jim said he chalked it up to his imagination and walked back to resume cleaning the carpet. "That's when I heard a bump behind me. I turned around, expecting to see Audrey but instead I saw an older male standing beside the popcorn machine dressed in something akin to a tuxedo and he looked just like he had reached in to get popcorn and had closed the door shut. But he vanished right before my eyes! Leaving behind the definite aroma of freshly made popcorn!" Jim said he was so stunned he didn't think of running, he stood there motionless and that's when Audrey came from the restroom and stopped in her tracks.

She looked at Jim and asked, "You're as white as a ghost. Are you feeling sick, Jim?"

Jim said he couldn't utter a word, he simply nodded confirmation that he felt sick. Audrey volunteered to finish his duties so he could leave, but Jim wouldn't leave. It took a while for him to regain his composure but he finally did and he finished his duties that night.

After that night whenever he was in the theater he caught himself looking over his shoulder and watching out for shadows or apparitions. Jim said he always felt the presence of someone watching him, "I don't know why the well-dressed man chose me to show himself to, but I wish he hadn't."

Jim admitted some of his experiences to the manager, hoping for confirmation from someone else that what he had seen was real, or not real, either way, he felt he finally had to speak up, "When I mentioned hearing odd noises and seeing shadows to the manager, he reminded me that it was an old building with good acoustics and any small noise would be amplified and practically impossible to tell where a sound was coming from. He also said that shadows were common in dimly lit places. Since he seemed sure of himself I couldn't tell him about the man I actually saw, he would never believe me. I definitely saw an apparition of an older, well dressed man." Jim didn't share his experience with anyone else for many years. He changed jobs that same year, citing a 'better opportunity' rather than a 'ghost' as being the reason he left the theater.

Jim didn't visit the theater, not even to see a movie until he had children of his own with whom to enjoy a family outing. One evening he took his family to the theater to see a movie. Jim explains, "Even though there had been some remodeling the layout was basically the same and when I walked in a more mature, wiser man I still caught myself looking around a bit, wondering if he was still there. Fortunately I turned my attention to the family night out and the movie. I didn't see anything or feel anything unexplainable. Still, as we were leaving I looked over my shoulder, half expecting to see him standing there, waving goodbye to an old friend, but I never saw him or anything like him again in my life. Nor do I want to."

Naturally this experience intrigued me as a paranormal researcher and author of ghost tales so I approached many people who had ties to the old theater, finally finding someone who had been inside the recently remodeled building. This man, whom I will name Seth didn't believe in ghosts or spirits but he was kind enough to speak with me at length about a story he had heard from a lady, whom I will name Lisa, he knew Lisa well and respected her. Lisa's sighting was eerily similar to Jim's experience, except it was decades later: Lisa was dropping off some supplies after hours one evening. She should have been alone in the building and believed herself to be. As she began walking towards the exit she suddenly saw an older, well dressed gentleman appear. Discovering him was very much a surprise, so Lisa spoke aloud to him in greeting as he approached, he took a few long steps before vanishing less than five feet in front of her. The entire incident lasted only seconds but it startled Lisa so much that she raced out of the building to her car in the parking lot. She noted that hers was the only vehicle in sight. She quickly phoned Seth, requesting that he come to the building, fearing someone was playing a prank on her. Once he arrived they both entered the building together, looked around the interior, confirming that they were locked inside the building totally alone. Seth believed Lisa, likewise I believe Seth.

Whenever I am driving by the building that once was a theater, I pause and gaze upon it, thinking about the feisty, well-dressed man who had made an appearance for Jim, then decades later for Lisa. I can imagine him working there long ago when it was a performance hall. Maybe he had been a prankster even then, accustomed to receiving attention and applause. After all, the old building was once notorious for entertainment, laughter, tears and emotion.

Other Proclaimed Haunted Theaters in Tennessee

Theaters seem to be particularly prone to paranormal activity. Theater people have long been aware of that fact. That is why, after a play or musical, when the work crew comes out to clean up, they place a large upright pole with a bare bulb in the middle of the stage. It is called a "ghost light" and it is not there for illumination, but to drive away the ghosts that come out when the audience leaves. Tennessee has a few theaters known to be haunted as well.

Orpheum Theatre
Memphis, TN.

Most of the seats at Memphis's Orpheum Theater are good ones. But you might want to steer clear of C-5. That's where there have been numerous sightings of "Mary," a see-through apparition of a female child, she is basically shy, but has been seen enjoying rehearsals and performances at this former vaudeville venue, she is especially fond of hearing the organ being played.

The Bijou Theater
Knoxville, TN

The Bijou was first built in 1817 as the Lamar House; the theater was not added until 1908. It began as a place where the Knoxville Opera and Symphony played. During the Civil War the Bijou was used as a hospital. Workers have reported hearing voices when no one is there, seeing apparitions and being touched by unseen hands. So don't be surprised to hear laughter and movements coming from the Bijou late at night. It might be a Civil War Colonel, former movie star, or maybe even a prostitute as

this building was once known as the best house of ill
repute many, many years ago.

The Tennessee Theater
Knoxville, TN

Currently there hasn't been a lot of research or
material released on the possibility of The Tennessee
Theater being haunted. However, I am friends with a
gentleman who works at the theater and he feels very
much inclined to believe there are several spirits roaming
the elegant and historical grounds, inside and outside the
theater.

Not one but several spirits have been seen
entering and leaving the auditorium, and one elderly lady-
specter frequents the ladies room. This entity seems a bit
melodramatic as she bustles down the corridor, rushing
through the lavatory door and sometimes the echo of a
stall door slamming closed can be heard.

Theaters do seem to be a frequent hot spot for
paranormal influences, and I for one had such a sighting
at the newest theater in Oak Ridge, TN. My next story
shares the brief but pronounced visual that both my
husband (at the time) and I saw on two separate visits.

Chapter 2
Paranormal Commotion
(Oak Ridge, TN)

I would be very interested in hearing from others who have experienced something unexplained at the current theater in Oak Ridge, because I am going on the record right now, suggesting that it very well might have ghostly visitors.

The first time we encountered a strange occurrence at the newer theater downtown, was when The Green Lantern was being aired. My son and his friend were inside theater room 4, while my husband and I saw another movie in a different auditorium.

Being the protective parents we are my husband Ron would check on the boys a few times during the movie, and on this particular day (yes, we usually went to the matinee showing to save money) there weren't very many audience members in either theater.

Ron returned to the seat beside me after his second check-in of the children and he leaned into me and whispered, "Remind me to tell you what just happened." I felt a moment of alarm but he put a finger to his lips signaling silence and we watched the movie without incident.

However, back in the car I asked Ron what he meant when he asked to be reminded of something that had happened in cinema number 4. He looked cautiously over his shoulder, both boys were playing hand held video games, their attention diverted, "Tammy, when I checked on the boys that second time I saw a young person seated two rows in front of them, as soon as I entered the theater he suddenly ducked down. His actions concerned me so I walked up to that row to look and there wasn't a person anywhere. I even checked a few of the surrounding rows and the only people I saw were sitting in their seats watching the movie quietly. There couldn't have been a dozen people in the whole room, so I know what I saw. It was the weirdest thing."

To be honest at that moment neither of us thought anything paranormal had happened. Especially Ron, he was much more skeptical than I. We both assumed someone had snuck in and was hiding and had been both deft and good at hiding.

Ron described the person as youth sized, maybe a young teen or pre-teen, and he said it made him very nervous so he actually checked in on the boys more times than usual, never seeing anyone in the three rows in front of our son and his friend. We didn't ask the boys about it at that time, we didn't want to alert them or concern them for any future showings where we all may not enjoy the same movie and might end up in different auditoriums.

The next odd occurrence would be two years or so later. It was at one of the Paranormal Activity showings, I can't recall if it was number 2 or 3, they all ran together for me. Again my son and a cousin were watching a different movie. My daughter, Ron and I watched the horror flick. Once again we were in a theater with fewer than 20 people in attendance and for certain no one was in the row in front of us.

This time I checked on the boys, but not as frequently because the cousin was older than both of our children so we felt our son was reasonably safe in the other auditorium.

While I was returning to my seat I distinctly saw a floppy haired person sitting in front of where I had sat, I noticed this because no one had been there prior. We usually prefer to sit middle of the theater many rows back, and as I ascended the stairs the person seemingly ducked down. My heart quickened, because I was looking straight at what appeared to be a light haired boy, maybe twelve to thirteen years old, and it's like he dived down quickly. I hastened my approach and looked down the row and low and behold, there was no one there! No one! And I could see well enough to make no mistake about his presence – or lack of. I stood there for a moment longer than I should have and my husband motioned for me to come on and take a seat.

I whispered to him, "Did you see that? Where did that boy go?"

Ron cast me a bemused glance and gave a disagreeing shake of the head.

"Seriously, where did he go?" I demanded.

Ron leaned close, "No one was sitting there, Tammy." His own odd encounter seemingly forgotten the day of the Green Lantern showing.

But I kept my peace and tried to resume interest in the movie, yet my attention was hampered by my intrigue with the mysterious movie goer. Needless to say, no one returned to the seat, no one stirred in front of us, I could not find a solution to the inexplicable disappearance of a young boy I saw very plainly.

Once again after the movie I brought the subject up and Ron insisted he had seen no one in that seat or that row. Our daughter, on the other hand admitted she had seen someone fitting the description enter the auditorium but she didn't watch where he went, but he did not sit down anywhere in front of us.

To this day when I visit this theater I am on high alert for any sighting that could be mystifying. I haven't seen anything peculiar there since, but it's probably because I watch for it more closely. Phantoms have a way of surprising us.

I know without a doubt what I saw was there and then was gone. I anticipate hearing more about this theater and possibly discovering it has ghostly tales associated with it in the future. Maybe I am one of the first to publicly reveal that I think it has great potential for being one of Tennessee's haunted theaters.

Chapter 3
Ghost Business
(Jonesborough, TN)

It would be challenging to deny the heavy feeling that permeates a room where there is paranormal phenomenon. There is an unsettling sensation that someone is watching you, or is next to you when you are in the presence of spirits.

Even die-hard skeptics admit that there is an 'electrical' ambiance inside a quaint little store on Main St. in Jonesborough, the oldest town in Tennessee. Notably Jonesborough has been named one of the most haunted towns in America.

During my research of Jonesborough I found 3 locations which met the criteria of being inhabited by a "ghost." I prefer the term "spirit" and I prefer to classify a location as having possible "paranormal" activity versus saying it is haunted, but to simplify it I will interchange the terms frequently. Let me share a most interesting story. I can't use the name of the business but let me say that if you do visit Jonesborough be certain you spend a little time on Main Street dropping in to browse the shops there, when you enter this particular store you will probably detect a sudden shift in mood, sensing a change in the quality of air as the temperature drops several degrees at times for no logical reason. If you're alone you will be tempted to look over your shoulder as you browse the merchandise, expecting to see someone watching you very carefully. It won't be the shop owner or the clerk, they are friendly people who will encourage you to stay as long as need to, or offer assistance, but they won't tail you as you make your way through the shop. A very sensitive person might identify who is watching them, and if a true psychic enters the store, well I have been told it is overwhelming the way the unseen inhabitant makes its presence known.

Jonesborough was founded in 1780, sixteen years before Tennessee even became a state. This particular building's construction dates back to the early to mid-1800's. The shop has been many things during the past two hundred years; likewise the apartments above the stores have survived countless residents.

The current shop owner realizes there is a specter present. Merchandise is often disturbed during the overnight hours while the shop is closed. "I'm not sure if this ghost just wants our attention or if we don't keep shop to suit it, but whatever the case may be, we can count on finding items in different locations upon opening the store at least once a month if not more often."

It's usually small, light-weight items and generally the item hasn't been moved very far. On a few occasions an item has been dropped to the floor and in some instances broken.

"However this is not a malicious spirit." The shop owner insists. "No one here has ever felt threatened."

Many of the customers think the spirit belongs to a young man who hung himself in the apartment above the store a very long time ago and of those who remember the man's story will greet the unseen presence by name. But the fact is, no one really knows who the spirit once was, only that it has been "felt" by many and "glimpsed" by a few.

"The oddest thing that ever happened was the evening we got a deep snow in the1990's." The shop owner recalls that the snow moved in before closing hours that day, "I decided to stay all night instead of risking the bad weather. I have a small television in the office and a comfortable place to rest. I had settled down after closing, and it gave me a chance to get the book work done. I was watching TV, but the screen kept flickering like it was going to go off or something. I thought the power might be about to go out but oddly the desk lamp didn't flicker. I contributed it to the weather so I sat there watching a boring show, admittedly dozing on and off for a little bit. I had fallen asleep, unaware of what was happening because all at once the television blared out a harsh, inert noise and the screen lit up from the obnoxious static display of a channel lost and I opened my eyes and saw the shadow of a man moving towards the TV., as if he was going to adjust it, I saw his shadowy arm reach out and then the television went off! I jumped up from the chair with the hair standing up on the back of my neck! All the while the shadowy figure kept moving, as if trying to figure out what was wrong with the television, and then it turned around and all but disappeared within a few feet from me! Right in front of my eyes!" The shop owner explains that he was uncomfortable the rest of the night but didn't have any other odd thing happen that night.

"After you stay around this place for a while it gets easier to live with it. Radio stations will drift and I know it's the ghost changing stations. Nothing alarms me anymore, I just ignore it and we go about our business."

What do the regular customers think about Jonesborough's Ghostly Business? There are definitely mixed reviews. The locals know the story and there are many who believe the shop is haunted, the majority of the customers take it all in stride acknowledging that it does raise the curiosity factor while they shop at one of their favorite local establishments. Several mention feeling as if someone is nearby, but out of the way as if watching them, they don't feel threatened. Of those who refuse to believe in ghosts they simply say the shop owner and his clerk are eccentric and have created the ghost story to generate more business. The customers who disbelieve sniffs at the preposterous idea of ghosts and admittedly they do not encourage the sharing of personal accounts of ghostly encounters.

Naturally, while researching the haunted legends of Jonesborough I met with the shop owner and visited the store. As per normal investigations, odd things do not immediately jump out at us, or strange noises do not suddenly interrupt our conversations. These things take time, and frequently requires follow up visits. One thing that was noticeable early on was that it felt cooler inside the store in certain spots, especially the back office and near the register. Not each time we were in those areas, but there was a marked drop in temperature more than once as we walked around those "cold spots" within the store.

Also, my EMF meter spiked erratically in a few places and without pattern. We didn't catch any voices during our audio recordings but we did see a fast orb in motion which darted from the front of the store towards the back during a video recording session. A large orb in motion isn't proof, but when we slowed the video frames down to analyze the movement we noticed that as the orb zipped by in its wake the bracelets and necklaces hanging on a display moved a little, as if something brushed by the corded merchandise with enough momentum to create a draft, or maybe a light skimming from the spherical energy of a ghost caused the movement which was visually detectable via video recording and more so when I deliberately slowed the playback speed.

In essence after we spent overnight in Jonesborough and visited several locations we captured enough unexplainable evidence collectively to encourage anyone who is interested in the paranormal to make a decision themselves. Visit the town, visit the stores and stay at one of the older Bed and Breakfast Inns or take a walking ghost tour. Chances are you won't be disappointed. I wasn't. I have several photographs of possible apparitions in the windows after night closes down the quaint town.

Chapter 4
Historically Haunted
(Harriman, TN)

"I personally *know* people who have seen angry- looking, male apparitions that appear suddenly, reaching out as if to touch you." Arnold is demonstrating with extended arms, reaching outwards, then he whips his hands upwards and sprawls his fingers over the air, "Then they simply vanish! Just that quick, you see them, then they're gone!!"

"Can you trust the people who have told you about this?" I asked.

Arnold nods with a determined certainty, "They have no reason to lie."

He's talking about the 121 year old Temperance Building in the quaint community of Harriman in Roane County. "Has this happened to visitors, or some of the personnel?" I gently inquire, never wanting to demean anyone's experience or story.

"I've known some of the workers and cleaning staff nearly a lifetime. They've all either heard doors slamming, or heard the heavy sound of walking, like boots pacing the floor, or strange voices coming from the upper part of the building. And if you don't believe me you can ask some of the established residents in Harriman, I've learned about several people who've witnessed apparitions staring at them from one of the windows in the old building. It was a jailhouse a long time ago, you know? And those apparitions, well they act like inmates reaching through the bars to get your attention."

It's easy enough to believe what Arnold is saying, I can imagine it in detail as many notable and colorful characters have graced the halls of the Temperance Building, which currently serves as city hall as of this writing, but has housed everyone from bootleggers to prisoners when it was a jail. It also had a short run as home to many small classrooms when it was the American Temperance University. It was originally the headquarters of East Tennessee Land Company, but early land deeds in Harriman required that the property couldn't be used to sell, store or consume alcohol which forced the land company out of business.

When I visited the building in 2010, I immediately detected that the ambience inside the building was thick and congested. This was during a time when I knew very little about the history of the place. I had initially visited Harriman to tour the older area resembling homes and buildings from another century. I'm speaking of the Cornstalk Heights district and the many Victorian homes which incidentally are my personal favorite architectural style of home. Initially I was intrigued by the old Princess Theater, immediately falling in love with the building. Unfortunately, I was unable to gain permission to get inside of the theater. But when I saw the Temperance Building I knew the place had potential to be haunted.

Once inside the building I captured some interesting photographs of distinct orbs on the stairs where I sensed a marked presence. Prior to entering the structure while waiting for my tour I busily snapped photographs of the exterior and discovered that one picture featured a hollow eyed, youthful appearing girl's face peering out from one of the windows. I can't be certain that no one was inside the building at the time when I snapped the photograph, but when I got to tour the inside an hour or so later there were only two men who let us in, there was not a female present, especially a young female anywhere to be seen. The mysterious photograph intrigues me, especially in consideration of our collective experiences inside.

Collectively "we" were one of my closest friends, my spouse and a few people who were also on the tour. Not only did each of us sense a presence and felt eyes watching us, we heard footsteps and what sounded like many whispers, just like Arnold described but the perplexity is that I wouldn't speak with Arnold until two years AFTER this visit, so I was there without influence from his story.

Since I was not there on a proper investigation I didn't have audio or video devices to capture the voices or footfall we all heard, however I did have various models of EMF detectors that evening and I experienced erratic Electro Magnetic Fluctuations in several locations inside the building, corresponding with the unexplained cold spots and the random feeling that something "brushed" by two of us. In the wake of the unexplained feeling that something swept by us my friend thought she heard a little girl's voice.

"Did you hear that?" She whirled around, and we both looked at each other. "Did you say something?" But she knew I hadn't and she bustled by me and retraced our steps. "I know what I heard." There was an edginess to her voice.

"What did you hear?" Our EMF meter responded by lighting up. We grew excited.

"It sounded like a little girl's voice, but I couldn't make out what she said. A few words, quick like." She was intent upon replicating the experience, we left the tour entirely so that we could hang back without interruption, there weren't that many people in the building, all of them were in front of us and none were children, but we didn't want to confuse the visitor noise with possible ghostly noise.

Neither my friend nor I realized then that I had captured what appeared to be a female child in the window of The Temperance Building in a photograph, not until I went through the pictures after the tour. The pictures of orbs on the stairs where I had felt a cold spot, the erratic emf display along with the unexplained noise/voice my friend heard which sound like a young girl or child in the absence of a youthful child in the building intrigued me in review of our visit later.

Shortly after my visit to the building I approached a council member to address having an overnight paranormal investigation to test my belief that the building was haunted, sharing our experiences with the girl's face in the photo and the child's voice my friend heard with the erratic EMF readings, but my friend and I were refused entry to investigate, possibly because they were already working with another local paranormal team, or possibly at the time they weren't open to such findings. However, I believed then as I do now that the old Temperance Building is haunted and I strongly encourage people to go to the Harriman Annual Ghost Tours, or the Christmas tours if it's still being hosted featuring a guided walking ghost tour through the Cornstalk Heights Historic District at Halloween that included the Harriman Temperance Building when we went. Either holiday is a great opportunity to visit the building and see the district that lured me there in the first place, if they still conduct these public tours.

If you do get to tour the old building, remember the story that Arnold shared, along with our brief experiences inside the place, perhaps you will hear, or see something unexplainable there as well. Take plenty of pictures, you never know what will show up when you look back on them.

_____

Are *Ghosts* even REAL?

That's an age-old question. Perhaps "ghosts" are in the minds of the believer.

Certainly, a large percentage of our population, approximately 45% believe in ghosts or spirits. Most people admit they have had weird sensations or have seen shapes out of the corner of their eye, only to discover it disappeared when they turned to look. Or have heard noises while being totally alone. Others have even been touched by unseen hands.

Paranormal researchers and experts in the field believe that the presence of spirits may be real. They also group the different types of spirits you may encounter.

Do different TYPES of *GHOSTS* exist?

Let's take a closer look at what the experts say:

The Interactive Spirit. This is the most commonly encountered ghost. This spirit will appear in the form of someone you knew, either a deceased loved one, or a historical figure. They can be friendly, or not friendly. They can reveal themselves in a variety of ways. Including appearing in the human-form you recognize. Or they may emit a familiar odor, such as your deceased aunt's favorite perfume, or your uncle's beloved cigar. They can also make noises to get your attention, or even touch you. Most of the time the interactive spirit vanishes almost as quickly as it appears, and seems to visit when you are going through an emotional period in life. Perhaps they are trying to reassure you that everything will be alright.

The Vapor or Ecto-Mist:

This is the type of ghost which commonly appears in graveyards or historic battefields, and usually appear as a swirling mist/vapor or cloud. They can be white, gray or black in color. They usually hover above the ground by several feet and can move swiftly, or very slowly, or not move at all. They can float away, upwards, or even vanish instantly, sometimes they even turn into full blown, ghostly apparitions. You may even feel a chill in the wake of a Vapor or Mist.

Orbs or Energy Globes:

Most commonly photographed, or caught on video, orbs can sometimes be seen with the naked eye. Not to be confused with dust particles or insects, true *"spirit orbs"* are balls/spheres of energy from deceased people or even animals which travel quickly from place to place. Most commonly pale in color, some will have a nuceleus-like center, which is perceived as being a stronger energy source. Other orbs may be blue, white, or tan, (we have even captured red orbs.) Many times orbs appear just prior to a full blown apparition or coincides with other paranormal noise, or energy. Pay attention, and don't be so quick to dimiss the spirit orb as dust or an environmental particulate caught by a camera.

Noisy Ghosts/Poltergeists:

Many researchers believe that poltergeists can cause harm, and therefore are considered to be one of more dangerous forms of a haunting. They have the ability to manipulate their environment. From slamming doors, to opening and closing windows, to throwing objects, you can see how alarming such a haunting would be, and you can only imagine the potential for harm. Not to be confused with a demon or demonic possession, a poltergeist is a powerful embodiment which may start out slow and infrequent, feeding off of the fear and energy of the living as it becomes stronger and more capable of causing injury. Although some spirits are "noisy", they usually can not lift heavy objects and typically do not destroy their surroundings, as a poltergeist is thought to be capable of. You will know if you have a poltergeist if you start to feel unwell, have violent feelings that are abnormal for you after being exposed to this type of haunting.

The Residual Spirit:

This is really not so much of a "haunting" as a recording or replay of a specific energy. Usually as a result of a very traumatic, untimely or vile demise, it is believed that a residual energy lingers, or is imbedded in the place where such an occurence happened. As a result of the lingering energy from the past, individuals in the future may get to experience seeing a type of "recording" of these events. The spirit in this case does not seem to interact, and seems oblivious to the surroundings, simply replaying an emotional or tragic event. The energy surrounding a *residual haunting* may be very heavy, but should not be feared. Even though you may hear noises, and may experience interruptions in electricity or electrical appliances, these spirits are harmless and often fade over a long period of time.

Chapter 5
The Witch of Old Goby
(Morgan County, TN)

Halloween is the most fitting time of the year to speak about ghosts, witches and otherworldly beings. Not everyone believes in ghosts, or witches for that matter, yet "witches" have been around almost as long as mankind. They were especially loathed and feared as evidenced by the witch trials of the early fifteenth and sixteenth centuries.

Ghosts, of course, have been around since the beginning of mankind - as one must live to die and must die to become a ghost, haint, shade or spook: thus when life began soon thereafter death ultimately followed and of course lingering spirits began to enter the dreams and visions of man. Ghosts, spirits, supernatural beings, choose your terminology, choose your belief, but *do* choose to read about the witch of Morgan County:

This story may not represent the common conception of modern witches or ghosts, it does recognize a fear that is deep seated in many common folk, especially those who know the astonishing tale about the Witch of Old Goby - and if the tale made this book, then ultimately she must now be a ghost.

Somewhere along a very rural road in Wartburg, TN there was a century old home nestled solemnly in a wooded area. (And I use the term "somewhere" very loosely. I know where it was, and I imagine the grounds are as inhabited by a spirit as the house once was. But my experience with sharing the exact locations of abandoned homes and churches and cemeteries have been all negative, as thrill seekers and amateur ghost hunters who have no respect for such places, thus visiting, stealing from, damaging and destroying such locations have now persuaded me to keep the exact location secret if it's empty, or abandoned, etc. unless there is previously published information already established.)

Back to the witch story: The original owner of the house, perhaps the only owner, died in the nineteenth century, yet the house stood longer than that. The paint peeled from the wooden exterior, the windows were cracked or missing completely, the porch planks were weakened from rot. The house captivated the interest of many young people - even mature persons couldn't resist the titillating tale that encompassed the house and its owner.

Teenagers and young adults considered it a rite of passage to sneak inside on Halloween. But such visits weren't limited to an annual holiday. Visiting the house in the dark of night suggested proof of certain bravery. Some curiosity seekers visited during the light of day when the sun cast a bright and warm ray of light upon the house, removing some of the feeling of forebode. Yet even in daylight the dark recesses moaned and creaked of something cold and disturbing.

The house sort of sat sideways from the road, a shambled reminder of days gone by, it was never updated to public water or sewer. Even when the old witch died the house was outdated for that specific era, today it would be a museum relic if it was still erect. Eventually the earth's overgrowth engulfed the structure, vines and shrub and young trees grew to protect it from curiosity seekers, from vandals, from writers and paranormal researchers like myself. Maybe the witch's curse did what the spell was intended to do, maybe the earth grew to shield her home from prying eyes keeping it sacred and protected from other human inhabitants. Until the climate and bugs and pests destroyed the structural support and it collapsed in upon itself, properly burying it, along with the charms and spells and secrets already buried in the ground around it.

There are numerous accounts from random people who saw her sitting on the front porch in an old rocking chair back in the nineteenth century. She was always older looking than her actual years so rumors insisted that she was in her hundreds even before she was a bona fide senior citizen. The fact is she died at the age of ninety. Few outsiders knew that, how could they get to know her when she was such an outcast?

Back when the locals saw her sitting on the porch there was no reason to wave, why would anyone dare wave at her when she had the ability to put a curse on someone? That was her reputation, that she would '"hex you".

Sadly enough there were a few people who would throw rocks at her house so unnerved by her presence they were. But for the most part the locals kept to themselves and avoided her on the rare occasion they encountered her in public. She was a quiet person who looked you straight in the eye but rarely spoke. When she did speak it was to the point, usually in direct response to a need or a question. There was no common courtesy yet no one could say she did anything out of malaise except for the people who blamed their misfortune on the witch.

She knew what people thought and said about her, and when people brazenly said unkind things she would snap. "Leave me alone." She'd say this, bravely meeting and holding their gaze, "Go about your business before you make me cross." Coming from a small framed, gray haired woman such a comment could only be taken one or two ways. If she wasn't carrying a gun then it made sense she had other means of ending such meddling, so rumors persisted for decades that she simply cursed whoever crossed her with a witch's spell.

After the old woman died no one claimed her estate. She didn't have heirs as she had never mothered a single child. Though she had been married once, her husband had prematurely died in his thirties and she never remarried. The witch had outlived her siblings and of course her parents, so the old house sat empty for more than a decade. The county tried to auction it off but there were no bidders. It stood silently among the trees and thickening vegetation and the animals eventually claimed it as their own.

Over the years scores of teenagers visited the dwelling trying to get inside the witch's house. They would park their vehicles nearby, it didn't have a driveway, she had never owned a car, and they would walk onto the front porch, only the bravest ever made it past the entrance. Several young people claim to have heard her rambling around inside the house, or heard her "ghost" to be exact, because remember this was long after the old witch had died. But the nay-sayers claimed such noises came from animals inhabiting the premises.

Of those who actually entered the structure many claimed that the inside was more eerie than the outside. Old, broken furniture dilapidated from years of being left to the elements cluttered the rooms along with old doilies and afghans musky from moisture and mildew. It seemed the woman was fond of cupboards and within the many cupboards were jars and jars of unnamed contents, perhaps herbs, perhaps concoctions made over a burning fire, but no one was fearless enough to try to determine what was inside the mason jars. The woman's bizarre housekeeping preferences fueled the rumors that she was indeed a witch.

In addition to these peculiarities was the very fact that most of the people who had gone inside seemed to coincidentally fall ill after trespassing. Most were afflicted with bronchial ailments or stomach upset. A few had very high fever that lasted for days. With such adverse reactions no wonder people feared the witch's cursed house. "Well maybe the illnesses were mere coincidences." You may say. "Indeed." I would concur, then challenge you to explain this very bizarre phenomena I am about to share.

Over the years as my reading audience has expanded and as people have become familiar with my intense fascination and research into ghost stories and folklore, I have encountered more than half a dozen people who have gone out to the Witch's House on Old Goby Road. Each person has heard or seen something unexplainable but the experience of one particular family fascinates me the most, as their group actually 'saw' the ghost of the witch.

At first as they approached the house they could see an old, brown rocker on the front porch. They looked at the house which once was painted white but now looked dirty and gray, the screen door hung from a single hinge and the windows were broken. It was obvious others had been inside before, the door gaped open as if allowing or inviting access. Two boys and two girls, all related, went inside cautiously with flashlights in hand. In spite of the dwindling day light the absence of natural light inside required artificial illumination. These are the young folk who described the interior of the house to me. They could hear things scurrying about in the attic and the girls wanted to leave as fast as they could but the boys were intrigued and wanted to probe into the closets and drawers, dismissing the sounds they heard as squirrels and birds. But no one could dismiss the distinct sound of the screen door banging on that single hinge. All four of the young people startled aloud and looked towards the entrance of the house. It was then that they saw a shadow beyond the window of the front porch.

"Someone is out there." Doug whispered.

They waited, listening intently and heard a couple of thuds and then the familiar, repetitive squeaky sound from a rocking chair swaying on a hard wood porch.

Randy pulled at Kate's arm and the other two followed as they crept as silently as they could towards the window and that's when they saw her profile, sprouting long, thin hair and the hunched posture of a distinctly elderly female sitting in the chair… rocking slowly.

"It's the witch!" Linda shrieked and all at once there was a whooshing sound after the old woman turned and looked at them through the filmy window pane, her eyes sharp and steely for the mere seconds that their eyes locked, then suddenly she disappeared from the chair which creaked beneath the weight of a vanishing figure.

The foursome stood dumbfounded and speechless for minutes on end and finally Doug found his voice, "Did we just see a ghost?"

"Let's make sure." Randy encouraged and lead them towards the door where they exited cautiously, watching for any movement. No one was there on the porch or anywhere in sight.

Their attention collectively focused on the old rocking chair now motionless. "That's literally impossible." Linda said, "We all saw her."

"Let's look around the house to be sure, you two go that way and we will go this way and meet in back." Randy suggested and quickly they separated and went in opposite directions, searching for sight or sound that could explain what they had seen. But they came up empty handed, except for one small item that Linda nearly tripped over at the corner of the house; it was an old mason jar, buried beneath the soil with just the top sticking up out of the ground. The foursome began to pull and dig until finally they broke it free. Caked with dirt and almost impossible to see the contents Doug began to shake his head, "I don't like this. After all, did you see all those mason jars in the kitchen?"

"I think we need to leave." Linda suggested not for the first time this evening.

"I can break it open to see what's inside." Randy offered.

But before he could attempt to break it open a noise caught their attention from inside the house. It sounded as if someone was rapping at a window pane.

All four looked towards the sound and even though it was now dusk they recognized the outline of thin, scraggly hair and the definite shadow of a human silhouette watching them from the kitchen window.

Randy dropped the mason jar and yelled for his friends to run! A second instruction wasn't required; they all hastened to get as far away from the creepy house as they possibly could!

This family was lucky as no one was injured during their departure, but another person I know who only made it to the outside claims he fell while stepping off the porch and broke his ankle, which he of course blamed on the witch's curse. He is also the one who believes that the mason jars were all various witches' bottles containing potions and items intended to cast spells.

No wonder the witch's house on Old Goby Road captivated the interest of those who seek out such locations for the stimulating anticipation of being frightened, or in my case for research into the supernatural and paranormal realm.

The Misconceptions of a Witch:

Having known many self-proclaimed and practicing Witches and Wiccans, I wish to take a moment to clarify that the previous story does not accurately reflect the reality of "Wicca" as a religion. Let it be known that when the elderly woman from the story was a young, practicing "witch", the term "witch" was more misunderstood than even now. In her day, the use of "wiccan" was most likely unknown and unused. (As referenced from the source www.licescience.com, Wiccan was founded in the early 1950's.) Although it's based on ancient beliefs, including aspects of paganism and nature-based spirituality, Wicca was founded by anthropologist Gerald Gardner in the early 1950s, according to "Magic-Religious Groups and Ritualistic Activities" (CRC Press, 2008). It is loosely based on Western European pagan rites and rituals that have been performed for centuries — before, during and after the time of Jesus — such as reverence of nature, observance of the cycle of the seasons, celebration of the harvest, and doing magic," according to "Wicca for Beginners" (Llewellyn Worldwide, 2006).

Also be aware that the words *witch*, *Wiccan*, and *Pagan* are used regularly, and interchangeably, but they're **not** all the same! Wicca is a tradition of **witchcraft.** Wicca is a religion whereas Witchcraft is a practice.

There is a great deal of debate among the Pagan community about whether or not Wicca is truly the same form of Witchcraft that the ancients practiced. Paganism is an umbrella term used to apply to a number of different earth-based faiths. Wicca falls under that heading, although not all Pagans are Wiccan. All Wiccans are witches, but not all witches are Wiccans. Finally, *some* witches are Pagans, but some are not - and some Pagans practice witchcraft, while others choose not to. Practitioners of "magic" are usually **Witches, and usually witches practice spell-work.**

Confused yet? So am I, but let me attempt to dispel some common myths:

Many people have believed that **Witches are evil.** That is simply **untrue.** Witchcraft and Wicca can be used in positive ways, Wicca opposes the use of negative, harmful magic and discourages people from hurting others physically or emotionally, practicing wiccans adhere to the Threefold Law, which believes that anything anyone wishes on another returns to them "three-fold".

As with any religion, there are followers who do dark things, or use their religion to conceal bad things, or use it towards negative purposes. Such witches who did **dark magic** and cast negative spells did exist, and still do. Those types of spells are known as voodoo. Perhaps this is one reason many people choose to believe that **Witches worship the Devil.** You may be surprised to learn that wiccans do **not** believe in the devil. Wiccans are often confused with **Satanists**. The concepts of the devil and hell are part of Christian theology and have never existed in the Wiccan religion, according to "Wiccan Beliefs and Practices" (Llewellyn Worldwide, 2001). Therefore, most wiccans, or witches do **not believe in the devil much less worship the devil.**

Another misconception is **that witches sacrifice animals**. Since Wicca is a nature-based religion, followers are encouraged to respect all living things.

The witch in our story was most likely a natural healer or so-called "wise woman" whose choice of profession was misunderstood, she was clearly a loner, eccentric and ostracized for her personal beliefs and practices.

Did the Witch of Old Goby cast a spell which protected her house, (even beyond her death)? Could such a spell be capable of making those who entered the house with bad intentions fall ill or face harm? It is a question that is still under debate.

Chapter 6

The Legend of K.G. Booger Hollow

(Loudon County, TN)

Do you know what total darkness is: The depth of blackness where you can't see your hand in front of your face? You can experience this complete lack of light deep in a cave with no lantern or flashlight. Or you can also experience pitch black darkness out in K.G. Booger Hollow, a long, winding stretch of road and land known to be rancid and plagued with evil. Out in the "Holler" you will certainly face your fears. Here in the south we sometimes say "holler" instead of "hollow". Regardless of how the word is written or spelled, "holler" is how I intend for it be conveyed for this story, alas I welcome you to the tale of *K.G. Booger Holler.*

The legend began more than one hundred years ago. Rumor is that this desolate stretch of backwoods road along with the land and woods surrounding it are tainted, the folk familiar with the area and the tales about it believe it to be true. Ask the locals if you dare, almost everyone within a fifteen mile radius has heard a story, or knows someone who has a tale to share. Not that there's many homes out there in the hollow in fact, there aren't many houses. That's why it's so tempting for thrill seekers to take a chilling ride in the dark of night to test their courage against the sinister ghost tales that have earned the old road which cuts through parts of Loudon and Roane County the name Knob Hollow, Black Hollow, Spook Hollow or K.G. Booger Hollow.

The first tragedy conveyed to me occurred more than a century ago when a young man named Luke W. was wrongfully accused of murder and was subsequently beheaded; his remains discarded in the woods as a vile reminder to everyone that "bloodshed begets bloodshed". His body was found a few thousand feet from his head which was discovered in one of the wells: A wishing well to be exact.

He became the accused when one of his drinking buddies was found shot to death after a public dispute occurred between the two men. Luke had begged for mercy and tried to convince the townsfolk of his innocence up until the very last minute when his arms were strapped behind his back and he was forced to his knees in front of a loathing group of witnesses, his final cry a hoarse, strained remnant of a voice slicing the cool autumn air, "Ye shall pay! Ye **all** shall pay by the very blood that shall soak this ground, the soil and water will turn sour as sure as I am innocent!"

Perhaps Luke's dying words held an unknown curse or maybe another force was at work because his prophecy came true. The water in the well soon lost its clarity and became odorous, unfit to drink. The land became sodden with an iniquity that made good men turn bad and bad men turn meaner.

On nights when the moon was bright and moisture clung to the branches of every tree, Luke's spirit could be seen roaming the musky, damp woods, sometimes visiting the wishing well. For more than thirty years his apparition floated here and yonder roaming silently in hopes that his innocence would be recognized. It roamed the holler for three decades until the real killer finally confessed.

On his deathbed, the real killer besieged with the guilt of both men's deaths laid heavily on Walter L.'s conscience, and he admitted he had been the one who killed Leonard C. He had witnessed the quarrel between Luke and Leonard that night, and even though he saw the men go their separate ways, he saw an opportunity. Walter had always hated Leonard, for the many indiscretions he perceived and believed about the man. He admitted that he had followed Leonard as the drunkard walked home, and when the opportunity presented itself, Walter had struck the man on the back of the head with a lead pipe, and as a result Luke had been accused of the crime and had died for it.

At last the ghost of K.G. Booger found some peace since it didn't haunt the woods for a while. Perhaps after death guilt burdens the living as the plague of wrong-doing weighs upon time itself, because as a result of Luke's dying promise many more lives were lost and more innocent blood was spilled, further spoiling the ground.

For years evil deeds were committed along the narrow, dirt road that was protected by the thickest of woods. Trees hundreds of years old shielded the ground by reaching for the light or maybe reaching for the heavens in hopes of redemption. Beneath the canopy of trees a darkness so intense that without a lantern man couldn't see where to take his next step and ultimately it was a place where death was easily concealed in these woods, as half a dozen bodies would be found over the next century - corpses rotting in shallow graves or discovered as skeletal remains.

The moans and whispers of restless spirits could be heard on any given night.

Icy, invisible fingers of the spirits seeking justice could be felt on the backs of anyone brave enough to walk the winding road. But few men dared venture into the 'holler' back in those days.

As newcomers began to build homes and raise cattle while farming fields these families soon discovered that crops wouldn't grow, cows would go dry and even worse the men folk seemed to slowly go insane. More than a few suicides happened out in K.G. Booger Hollow. Sadly a few women paid the price for the wickedness that seemingly seeped into the souls of their husbands.

One unlucky lady named Lily would become the next legendary ghost. Lily had been a hard working woman all of her life, helping her husband tend the farm. Soon loyalty and hard work wasn't enough to appease her husband who had grown sullen and quick tempered after they relocated to K.G. Booger Hollow. "We're growing poor out here in these god-forsaken woods!" He shouted when the crops become rancid and yielded very little. Each evening it was the same routine, Lily watching quietly while her husband sat sharpening his knife in front of the open hearth, growing increasingly agitated.

Lily voiced her concerns to her female friends explaining how he sharpened knives or axes every evening, grumbling about their situation while never acknowledging her when she tried to console. It also bothered her how often he would stand on the porch overlooking the land, his face long with disdain as he watched the wooded area beyond their home.

One evening Lily worked up the nerve to ask him, "What are you looking at, Wayne?"

At first he didn't seem to acknowledge her. As she turned to go inside the house he said, "It's not what I am looking at, it's what I am looking *for*."

"Oh?" She paused," What are you looking *for*?"

Wayne grunted, "Looking for what I saw at the well. I'm waiting for it to come back. Seen it a few times already… not sure what it is. About the size of a man, only it ain't a man." His voice held the slightest hint of uncertainty.

Lily shuddered and conveyed this to her friends saying that something about his demeanor had made her blood run cold. But it would be her friends who would shudder later, recognizing how Lily must have felt when she saw something peculiar about her husband's behavior, because they would eventually see it for themselves.

As weeks turned into months Lily felt more helpless as her husband rambled incessantly about how useless the land was. When Lily suggested they move away and start anew, Wayne became angrier, one time slapping her so hard she fell to the floor.

Wayne told her, "No use in leaving this place, it has already ruined us! Now get up off the floor and make yourself useful."

Lily admitted he was not the man she had married. She also admitted she was thankful they had not conceived a child in consideration of how things had changed in their marriage, which had also grown sour, she couldn't imagine bringing a child into their home. This would be Lily's last spoken disclosure.

It is common knowledge that what happens in secrecy sometimes stays a secret and Wayne never told exactly what happened. The only thing he ever spoke of was to the Sheriff when he was finally arrested for the murder of his wife. But few would give credence to what he said. Hardly any believed the incredible story of the night Lily carried a bucket of water up from the well. When she came up the hill Wayne was chopping wood. He said he saw Lily carrying the water bucket but he saw someone following her so he stopped and watched and as she got closer it became apparent that the person following her didn't have a head, so he shouted out a warning to his unsuspecting wife, but instead of looking behind her she changed direction and came towards him. Then, as she got closer Wayne said he could see **why** she was being followed and it was a horrible sight. "Here came Lily carrying a human head in the water bucket!" Wayne testified, "I could even see the whites of his eyes as they rolled around looking for the rest of him!"

Wayne said he started yelling at her to drop the bucket, shouting and screaming while trying to scare off the headless *thing*, trying to convince his wife not to carry the head towards him or their house. "She never was good at understanding!" He confessed but those words were the nearest to an admission the sheriff ever got. Wayne insisted that he didn't kill his wife. He swore that he had swung the axe at the headless "thing" but hadn't killed anyone.

The last thing he recalled was trying to run to safety inside his house. It was *he* who found Lily's dismembered body and it was *he* who called the sheriff, "If I had killed her wouldn't I have surely buried her body in the woods like others have done and not called the law?" He had challenged. Oddly enough not a drop of Lily's blood was found on Wayne or the clothing he claimed he was wearing at the time, not a drop was found inside the home, but her blood coated the axe and soaked the ground where she lay, obviously someone had killed her. A few days later one of Lily's hands was found inside the well: The same wishing well where Luke's head was discovered long before.

It seems Lily's spirit wants recognition because on some nights you can hear a woman screaming- not one shrill scream but a dozen shrieks of terror! Others say they have seen the ghost of a woman at the wishing well, but to this day no one has been brave enough to see what is in the bucket as the phantom female hoists it up the rope. The belief is that the two legendary ghosts now work together to scare trespassers: Lily hoisting Luke's head from the depths of the well. This is the reason dozens of brave people venture out into the holler – K.G. Booger Holler – to challenge the ghosts and the evil that lurks there.

If you're familiar with the area and brave enough to go there, look for Knob Road, if the road sign hasn't be stolen again or the road name hasn't been changed. Be wary of locals and protective land/homeowners, though, they often carry firearms and watch this area carefully, just be sure to park near the wishing well where a hand- carved sign beckons:

Welcome! Many years the well still stands-
Touched by many, many hands.
Oh the stories this well could tell –
If secrets spilled from our wishing well.

Chapter 7

The Haunted Field
(Wartburg, TN)

The sedan rolled slowly to a stop, the gravels and road debris crunching beneath the wheels as the two occupants looked silently towards the field, their eyes trained for the slightest of movements. The vehicle in appearance was an innocuous family car, but the women inside weren't out for a family drive on this warm, clear night.

"It's a full moon night." Doris noted aloud.

Amanda rolled her eyes, "Yep. It happens every month."

"You don't understand. This is a super moon, one of the brightest, clearest moons this year which should give us a better chance of seeing his ghost."

Amanda's focus turned once again to the field. She had lived in Wartburg her entire life, had driven by Chester Field countless times. Though she had not witnessed his apparition, her aunt Doris had. Her aunt was not a person to fabricate stories, not that anyone in the family thought she would.

Amanda asked, "So – what do we do now?"

Doris deftly leaned forward and pressed the button to open the trunk, "We are going to wait. Come on, I have insect repellent in the trunk and I brought the foldable chairs."

Amanda accompanied her Aunt to the rear of the vehicle where they both sprayed their clothing with insect repellant, gathered flashlights, a backpack and two foldable chairs. "How do you know where to go?"

"With this bright moon," Doris tossed a glance at the large orb in the sky, "it won't be too hard at all."

"Yeah, but I thought ghosts like the dark and I can see for miles, I really think this will be a waste of time."

Doris glanced again at the large moon then back to her car, mentally recalling the exact location. "This is practically the same time of night when I saw his apparition. I was parked on the side of the road near this same spot." Doris had pulled over that night because she felt a thumpity-thump, she got out of her car to walk back to inspect the rear tire. "When I saw I had a flat tire I felt a moment of panic." She related, after all it was late at night and she was alone, "But at least I had my cell phone." She was leading the way through the field, recounting her experience to Amanda. "I never thought about seeing a ghost that night, all I thought about was getting help and getting home safely."

The tall stalks of grass and weeds were damp and even though the females wore pants they both could feel moisture penetrating the fabric. Did this add to the coolness which enveloped them both?

Doris continued speaking after a momentary pause, "I called Randy and decided to wait inside the car until he arrived. Since it was a full moon night I could see the field very well, but it wasn't as bright as this. When I first saw the shadowy movement I thought it was my imagination, I didn't even try to invent an explanation for what I saw. But a movement kept catching my eye - I believe it was over there." She stopped in motion and used her eyes to point to where she felt they should go. "I saw a man, a definite manly shape and he was carrying something over his shoulder. I watched him walk towards the road, sometimes losing sight of him. But I watched him for several minutes and actually thought he might be walking towards my car. I turned on the hazard lights and it seemed he stopped moving. He stood still, but his figure wasn't as apparent anymore, it seemed more difficult to define, so I started to concentrate harder in an effort to see what was happening." Doris looked back at her car again, trying to decide if they had walked far enough.

Amanda looked at the vehicle also. "I don't think we should venture too far away, in case we have trouble I would like to be able to get back to your car quickly."

"I think we can stay here for a little while." Doris decided, dropping the back pack and chair onto the ground.

She and Amanda unfolded their chairs and placed them side by side. "It sure is a beautiful moon." Doris observed after taking a seat.

"Why would the moon have significance other than you saw him on a full moon night?"

"Because, he usually killed on full moon nights." Doris stated matter of fact, as if unbothered by the legacy the killer had left behind. After that fateful night when Doris had a flat tire, she went home and told several people what she had seen. She later learned there had been a man who had killed several women out there, on that same stretch of road, in the same field where she now sat in wait, when it had been a large farm and farmhouse a long time ago.

"How many bodies were discarded out here?"

"I never found out." Doris admitted. "It wasn't until he murdered his boss's daughter, the original land owner, before anyone knew about any killings." Doris had tried to research the stories and found very little published material about it, but she did find an article in the local newspaper archives, briefly describing how a servant had murdered his employer's only daughter, before being gunned down by the father. "He was carrying her bleeding body across this field towards the barn when the family dog followed them part ways, finally barking an alarm which brought the father with his loaded shotgun out to investigate."

Amanda's eyes scanned the field. The barn was long gone as was the original farm house, but she could imagine it. She could visualize a man, a trusted servant carrying a young woman who had shunned his advances, carrying her corpse over his shoulder leaving a heavy blood trail, maybe the hound dog had followed the trail or maybe the animal had seen his owner murdered. "He stabbed her to death?" Amanda inquired.

"Many times." Doris confirmed. Both women scanned the horizon, the fresh smell of nature momentarily lulling them into a calm state of mind. They sat for at least an hour, each lost in her own thoughts. Doris glanced at her watch, "It's past midnight, later than when I saw him."

"Doris, that was probably a once in a lifetime thing." Amanda resolved, "Do you really think you can see a ghost a second time?"

Doris didn't seem to doubt that she could, "After I started researching this property I discovered that a lot of people have seen his apparition, that's how I discovered the history because enough people have seen the specter and reported it." Doris gave a visible shudder. "Maybe he won't come through tonight, since

we are waiting for him, but I saw him clearly."
She had never revealed to her niece before this
night that she had already seen the ghost twice,
"I even saw him that night after Randy arrived
and was working on my flat tire. I kept watching
the field when suddenly a shadow figure raised
up from the grass much closer to my car than
before, he was looking straight at me and that's
when I let out a noise which caught Randy's
attention. Before I could point at the man the
apparition simply disappeared. Randy saw no
one, but I did. I saw him." Doris looked at her
niece with a sincere expression. "I knew then
that he was a ghost. I knew I had to find out if
anyone had died here in this field. Sure enough,
not only did the killer die here because the
father shot him, but his victims were all buried
here."

In an article published months after the
original newspaper write up, Doris found
another brief column with the headline,
"Skeletal Remains Found Buried at the Chester
Farmhouse after Daughter's Brutal Slaying."
The article revealed that investigators had
found random skeletal remains in shallow
graves, but most of the bones had been carried
away or consumed by wild animals. The report
stated that more details would be forthcoming,
but Doris never found another article published
about the identities of the bodies during her
research.

Amanda wrapped her arms around
herself and looked around on this bright full

moon night, "I haven't heard the slightest movement, or seen anything, Doris. When can we leave?"

Doris sighed at her niece's impatience. She had parked by the field on a few prior occasions, she and Randy trying to see a ghost, but it had never panned out. She had looked online and researched the most likely times when paranormal activity might be stronger, the consensus was that on full moon nights the air might be more saturated with positive ions, plus the added gravitational pull on the earth should be stronger during a full moon. There appeared to be an almost indisputable belief that the full moon resulted in an increase in paranormal phenomena. Pair that with the fact she had witnessed an apparition on a full moon night Doris was convinced she would see his ghost again on this specific night. "I guess we can leave now." Doris resigned, "I know what I saw. I will never forget it."

"Well, I don't want to burst your bubble but we have been out here more than an hour and it's as quiet as it can be. Besides, if you did see the ghost, what would you do?"

"Ghosts can't hurt us." Doris stated, standing to gather her belongings. She lifted the back pack which contained some items she had learned would help detect spirits. "We didn't even use any of these things."

"If a spirit isn't here those gadgets can't

detect a presence. Besides, you brought a camera and never got it out, either." Amanda reminded.

"You're right. Well give me a minute so I can take some pictures. At least our trip won't be a total waste of time." Doris unzipped the back pack, brought out the camera and began taking panoramic shots of the field. Doris had dozens of similar pictures back at home, always attempting to catch evidence the field was actually haunted.

After a few moments the ladies carried their possessions back to Doris' car and stuffed all of it back inside the trunk. Amanda asked, "Are you disappointed?"

"Yes, of course I am. But Randy once reminded me that a watch pot never boils. On the night I saw his apparition I wasn't expecting anything to happen. Maybe the spirit senses my desire to see him again. Who knows, maybe it was a once in a lifetime experience." They both got inside the car and Doris started the engine, slowly she began to pull away from the field onto the roadway.

Amanda's eyes were drawn to the field once again, the silvery moon beams creating a view so beautiful and peaceful it was hard to ever imagine such tragedy had occurred there. Suddenly she saw a darkened shape interrupt the serene vision and her pulse hastened. Her lips parted and words almost made it through her constricted throat but the revelation of what she was looking at rendered her speechless.

Just as her Aunt Doris had described Amanda saw his silhouette there, standing near the spot where they had been sitting moments earlier. He was facing their direction and she could feel him watching their departure, she could feel the stare from eyes she could not see. "D…D…Doris." She finally uttered, but it was then too late, she had moved her eyes for an instant and when she looked again he was gone.

"Did you say something?" Doris asked.

Amanda sat cold and silent, stunned and excited. But the truth was she didn't want to tell her Aunt, she didn't want to risk the chance that Doris might want to return to the field to see the ghostly visitor.

The horrible feeling that came after seeing the darkened apparition left Amanda with a troublesome thought, "I'm glad to get away from here. It doesn't give me a good feeling knowing what happened."

Doris uttered a quick agreement, recalling how she had felt that night she saw him. But the heavy burden that came with knowing what had actually taken place after Doris did some research was an even darker feeling. The feeling that came with this knowledge haunted Doris as much as having plainly seen the spirit of the killer.

Silence fell between them, each was thinking about an unbelievable image they both had seen, thinking about the dark apparition of a killer who still haunted a placid field in Wartburg. His dark, evil, tormented form carrying the limp, ethereal figures of those he had slain, those he had discarded in a field which occasionally reveals secrets to those unknowing passersby, the horrid past of bloodshed that is now known as a "killing field."

Chapter Eight

Campbell County's Angel

Any emergency worker can captivate us with inexplicable tales and intriguing experiences during their time working to serve our community. Most first responders have dealt with accidents and death, and tragedies beyond our scope of realization. I have talked with several emergency responders who can shed a new perspective on the deceased and the dying. Here is just one experience of a first responder's encounter with the ghostly figure of a drunken man.

Welcome to Campbell County, TN where most of the road ways are either narrow, curvy or treacherous with uncounted blind spots from numerous hills. Kevin, a young paramedic recalls the night he worked a horrific wreck on Bluff Rd.

Although Kevin was relatively new at the job, having worked just under a year, he had worked plenty of accidents, several with fatalities, but this one would never leave his mind. "This accident involved a family, three children and both of their parents. It had been raining and the road was challenging to navigate even under dry conditions. We are not sure why the mini-van left the road but it went off the road on a sharp curve and ended up taking down some small trees before coming to rest on its side, smashed up against a large tree."

Kevin pauses as he pulls in his breath, still visibly shaken from the memory of this particular accident, "When I got the call I was at a convenience store fueling the ambulance, my partner Jessica was inside the store buying a couple of soda's for us. The call came in at 11:31 pm., someone had seen the van's tail lights down over the embankment, and police were in route. Usually the fire truck will beat us to an accident scene, but somehow on this night Jessica and I were first to arrive at the location

"Since there were no witnesses when we arrived, no one knew what actually had happened, and the person who had reported the accident to the 911 operator had simply stated that an ambulance was needed, reporting that it would be impossible not to have injuries… or worse". Kevin said he could barely see the hint of the red tail lights when they arrived, in fact he and Jessica had slowed to a crawl and both were straining to see where the accident had occurred, the van was so far over the steep embankment. "This road was mostly absent of homes and there was not a real landmark or mile marker to distinguish where the van was located, so it wasn't easy finding the van. It was pure luck that anyone had seen the wreckage to report it since they hadn't witnessed the accident themselves."

It was a chilly November night, the temperature hovered at 40 degrees. Earlier in the day it had rained heavily now it was a mere drizzle and visibility was low, limited by a heavy misty fog. Kevin guided the emergency vehicle as safely out of the main roadway as he could, inwardly wishing another emergency responder would arrive. He looked at Jessica, "I think we need to try to determine how many are inside the van before we get our equipment."

They pulled on ponchos and vinyl gloves, carrying only one emergency bag at first.

Jessica had radioed dispatch notifying them that she and Kevin were first on the scene, she was informed that police and firefighters were less than five minutes away.

"How do we get down there to them?" Jessica asked as they cautiously attempted descending the embankment. Due to the intense foliage it was impossible to tell how deep the descent was. A large flashlight revealed the van left tire tracks in the vegetation approximately knee high. "Maybe walk in the tire tracks?" Kevin suggested.

The smell of lost fluids from the van sliced the muggy aroma of earth and the tail lights beckoned for them to hurry. Jessica and Kevin walked carefully, unsteadily, at times slipping as they treaded towards the van. Both Jessica and Kevin called out to anyone who may be able to respond, but they heard no cries for help, no moans of pain.

Hopefully the van had been occupied by the driver only and that person was knocked unconscious, but the closer the pair got to the vehicle the more apparent the damage became. The van had plowed over thin saplings, probably slowing its decent and possibly contributing to it rolling over because half way down the hill it had flipped over and Jessica and Kevin were no longer following tire tracks. The van's front had taken most of the impact but thankfully the motor prevented the tree from meeting the windshield, yet most of the windows were broken upon impact or from the roll over so the potential for severe gashes and internal injuries was likely.

"I hear sirens." Jessica said, her voice hopeful. She paused momentarily, silently asking Kevin if they should continue or wait for help. Technically they were supposed to wait for the firetruck, but considering the emphasis on the van's damage and the cold, wet environment Kevin had made a decision to proceed. But no one had responded to their voices when they called out.

"My gut told me that it was probable that the van had more than one passenger, and so I wanted to get to the van to be sure no one was bleeding to death, seconds count in situations like this."

The pair was now within visual of the van's interior with the flashlight Kevin directed over the full length of the van. "I see someone." His steps hastened, it wasn't easy walking through the wet, slippery vegetation, each step was uncertain, there were many rocks, stumps, and holes to impede their attempt to reach the occupants quickly. Jessica and Kevin both had nearly fallen multiple times

Kevin shouted out, "Are you alright? We're here to help. Can you hear us?" Again, only silence, just the sound of the couple's steps, whose only intent was to help.

When Kevin and Jessica kneeled down they could see that the parents were strapped in with seatbelts, both were clearly non responsive. A small body was also in the backseat, safely secured in a child's car seat. Both Jessica and Kevin inwardly hoped this little person was okay but he or she wasn't responding either, and blood covered his or her hair and face. It was a disturbing sight this small person who couldn't be more than four years old with matted hair sticking to the small, round head.

Jessica was on her knees, oblivious to the broken glass. "In situations like this the adrenaline pushes us past discomfort and minor injuries we may receive."

Kevin saw the strobing red lights of the firetruck approaching, hearing the sirens wailing. He could have waited for help but as he looked at the child, dangling from the car seat, all that mattered to him was helping Jessica reach the child. She was extending her full body into the van through the shattered side window.

Suddenly from behind him Kevin heard steps approaching, he pulled his eyes from the scene of Jessica reaching into the van, he was shocked to see a man approaching, his clothes soaked as he peered at Kevin beneath the rim of a camouflage cap. His face was a mask of panic, eyes wide.

Kevin looked at the man, searching for visible injuries, assuming he was another passenger of the van. "Help, need help." The man said, and quickly turned back from where he had come.

Kevin looked at Jessica, her fingers were on the carotid artery of the child, "What's the stat?"

"Weak pulse." She muttered.

Kevin was torn, but the fire truck was safely parked up on the roadside and the crew was now descending the embankment. "Down here, we have a young child with a weak pulse!" He yelled up, "And two adults appear unconscious!"

The man who had approached Kevin had paused and yelled back over his shoulder, "Save these children!" He shouted.

Kevin looked back at him, the face that had appeared panicked was now hardened with impatience. "I'm coming." Kevin yelled out, he looked back at Jessica, "I am going to find these other children."

Kevin had to walk quickly to catch up to the man who was trekking much better than he was. The children the man spoke of were at least 75 feet from the van, two small crumpled bodies almost lost in the knee high vegetation. Oddly Kevin noted that they were side by side, almost touching. The man hovered over their bodies, hastening Kevin with hand motions to hurry up.

Kevin knelt beside the children, they were bleeding badly and shards of glass projected from one of the children's side. He quickly assessed that they were indeed alive, but barely. He turned to the man, who had escaped any injuries. "Stay here, let me get help."

"There's no time. Grab her." Kevin instructed, pointing to the female, possibly 5 years old, her bloody hair a tangled mess around her face.

Kevin hoisted the child into his arms, cradling her limp form as he stormed through the foliage, unaware of any obstacles in his way, it was as if something was clearing his path ahead of him because he didn't stumble, slip or fall as he had coming down the hill. He didn't notice the man behind him whom he assumed had grabbed the male child, who had appeared to be a little older than the female he carried. Her body was already deathly cold, and her lips were turning blue. All Kevin could think about was getting her to the ambulance as quickly as possible. He was so focused that he couldn't hear the sirens of the police cruisers as they arrived. He couldn't hear the voices of the men and women shouting down at him. He could see the other emergency workers as they carried the youngest child up the hill on a mobile stretcher.

"Down here! Help us! This one is almost gone!" he shouted. "Call in life star!"

But that decision had already been made. When Kevin reached the two paramedics meeting him halfway he instructed them to grab the boy behind him. It wasn't until he saw their bewildered exchange that he finally looked back over his shoulder, expecting to see the man carrying the male child. Panic washed over him anew, and he handed the female child to the awaiting paramedic, "I know where he is. I will be right back."

Kevin was in his own zone, determined to save the boy, retracing his path perfectly, "I can't describe it any other way than to say that it was like there was adequate illumination, the grass that had been knee deep which had slowed mine and Jessica's descent was no longer a problem, I didn't step in holes or stumble over the rocks like I did on the way down, I went down that hill as if guided by an unseen presence. And when I got down there near the boy I could see the man hovering over him, still hastening me with his arm movements, telling me to hurry. I did wonder why he didn't carry the boy up behind me, but you know what? I just wanted to save those kids, I wasn't asking those kinds of questions."

It was at this moment that Kevin's voice caught in his throat, and he dropped his head as he continued telling the story weakly, "Three children were orphaned that night." He pulled in his breath raggedly, eyes now lifting upwards, skywards, and in his mind who knows what he was thinking, or saying to the heavens. "And the little girl I carried up the hill, she was in critical condition for 5 days. But she made it. All of the children made it." He was shaking his head positively, his voice growing stronger, "They made it because they had a guardian angel that night.

"The child in the car seat who Jessica rescued was 3 years old. He survived, I think he stayed in the hospital three days. The boy at the bottom of the hill was 7 years old, and he was in pretty bad shape, he spent two nights in critical care and was moved to a room for an additional 3 nights. But the girl child I carried, she was hospitalized for 14 days after being in critical care. The fact is, she died while in my arms but I didn't know it at the time. But the paramedics never stopped working on her and for that reason she is alive today." Kevin pauses again, for a lengthy moment, "And because that man was by their side, and comforted them, and came to me to get help, staying with the children until we got to them…" Kevin's voice softened, and his words caught in his throat, "If it wasn't for him we might not have found them in time, we didn't know to look for two children who had been tossed from the van, through the windows… they were cut up so badly, and they both had internal injuries. The girl had a severed liver… but the man, he got help and he stayed by their side… Except he wasn't a man."

This is where Kevin's voice gets excited and his eyes widen and his cheeks flush, "He wasn't there at all. I saw him, I talked to him, and I saw him as real as anybody there that night, but nobody else did. Nobody saw him, even when they went down the hill to get the boy with me, a man wasn't there, and Roger was right behind me and he said there was nobody there except the little boy lying in the grass. But I know better, that man didn't leave that child's side the whole time I was down there, yet nobody else saw him… except Kenzie." A half smile lifts the corner of his mouth, "The little girl, that was her name, you see I called or visited the hospital every day to check on them. And one day the grandparents wanted me to come in her room so Kenzie could personally thank the man who held her hand and sang to her…." His eyes brimmed with tears, "She was a little disappointed when they brought me in. She knew me from my visits as the man who drove the ambulance, but I wasn't the man she wanted to thank." For a moment Kevin can't continue, his emotions were so raw, but he finds his voice, "Kenzie didn't say a word, just looked at me quietly. I smiled at her, patted her little hand which was bruised and still had scabbing scratches on it. I told her I knew which man she was talking about, an older man, wearing camouflage. Her eyes widened and she seemed hopeful and I told her he was wearing a hat." Again Kevin is nodding positively as he tells the story, "She said, 'yep, that's him! He held our hands and told us we would be alright and he sang to us.'" Kevin paused to catch his breath, his face a mask of pure awe, "I have to tell you, her words made me cry out loud, but I didn't want to scare her so I laughed and told her to be glad it wasn't me singing to her, I sounded like an old barn yard cat with its tail caught in a door."

Kevin is again looking upwards, eyes misty but appreciative. "There was a guardian angel there that night." He said affirmatively. "Kenzie and I both saw him."

When asked if he ever knew of a man who had died at that same spot, possibly a hunter since he was dressed in camo, Kevin responded, "I already thought of that. But no, I can't verify if there ever was."

No verification is needed, Kenzie and Kevin both saw the man and interacted with him. The fact remains, first responders had no idea how many passengers were in the van, valuable time would have been lost if it hadn't been for the guardian angel pointing Kevin in the direction of the two injured children.

Chapter 8

A Ghostly Disturbance
(Heiskell, TN)

It goes without saying that strange things seem to happen more often during a full moon phase. Compare emergency room records for at least 28 days and you might be surprised how ER visits and hospital admittances increase as the full moon approaches. Speak with your local police officer about the cycle of crime and ask if it's possible that the rate of public disturbances, domestic violence and/or arrests increases near or during the full moon. I can promise you that if you ask a certain police officer in Anderson County you will be shocked at the full moon encounter he experienced several years ago.

Henry had worked for the police force for fifteen years in Anderson County prior to the peculiar incident which you will read about here.

Even though his job was most definitely stressful and often depressing the inherent perk was that he was able to protect those who needed protection, he believed that he and his entire police force made a difference in the lives of the average citizen. He was a proud man and a man in whom you could place trust.

Henry doesn't enjoy talking about that fateful full moon night, but he told me the story because he knew I chased ghost stories and he had a very interesting ghostly tale to share, one in which I took particular interest because I had encountered an apparition a decade ago on the very road where his encounter happened.

Henry was working the night shift and it happened to be a full moon night in September. He preceded the story with this very revealing fact, "I never liked working the crazy calls, especially when it was a full moon." He told me, "But, on the night in question I was the one who responded to the call. I was just a few miles away from the Heiskell volunteer fire department when this call came in to dispatch, someone reported a drunken man staggering alongside the road acting in a manner which alarmed the person prompting the call to dispatch. It was protocol that another officer would be in-route to assist me since violence could be an issue when dealing with intoxicated persons. I was close to the location so I decided I would drive out to take a look."

Keep in mind that the area and the road is very rural and although there are a number of houses in the vicinity they aren't tight knit and most houses are set back off the road a good distance. Henry believed that the suspicious male was probably a resident who was drunk and making a scene. As he drove the cruiser cautiously towards the vicinity where the caller claimed to have seen the person Henry turned his spotlight on and scanned the tree line, careful not to aim the bright light towards a residence.

Henry didn't see anyone anywhere, which surprised him since he had responded to the call almost immediately, arriving at the location within two minutes of the call. So Henry turned around in a driveway and slowly back-tracked his route, stunned to suddenly see what appeared to be the outline of a pair of legs walking on the side of the road from where he had just passed a moment earlier. He caught sight of the person in the beam of his headlights so he switched the spotlight on and aimed it at the back of a man revealing an image that made him wonder if it was a man at all.

"I had one of the strangest sensations run through my body when the bright spotlight illuminated this character," Henry explained, "He was walking away from me, he was wearing boots and jeans yet he was wearing a short robe, like a woman's night robe, sort of silky. And he was wearing a cowboy hat. It was so bizarre that I hesitated to hit the siren, but since he didn't seem to realize I was shining a light on him and following him in the police car I quickly blasted the siren for a split second. That man didn't even startle. He just kept walking in a staggering manner..." Henry felt goose bumps spill onto his arms and he felt the hairs on the back of his neck rise up. "I knew something wasn't right so I radioed into dispatch and explained that he was acting very peculiar and said I was going to turn around and come back towards him to get a better look." Henry said that the other officer was a few miles away at this point.

Henry eased his car into another driveway, watching the strange traveler carefully as he did so. The man simply walked without hesitation or reaction to Henry's police car presence and strobing lights. The oddly dressed man was walking as though dazed, but his very essence left Henry feeling unnerved. "There was something very strange about the man. I pulled the car onto the roadway and approached him again. This time I used the loud speaker and I called out to him, asking him to 'stop walking'."

The oddly dressed man didn't stop – he vanished. Henry thought his eyes were playing tricks on him, the man couldn't have disappeared. "I stopped the car exactly in the spot where the man had been walking and I panned the spotlight over the ditch line and the grassy area, looking for any sign of him. All of a sudden I felt like a cold vapor went through me when I realized there was no where he could have gone." Henry waited for his fellow officer before he stepped out of the cruiser. He was much shaken to say the least.

The other officer arrived within a minute, together they got out and shined their lights along the grass, the ditch line and up and down the roadway, they both drove in opposing directions along the road searching for the man, but there wasn't a drunken man, or any type of disturbance to be found. Unless you believe Henry's encounter to be a paranormal disturbance. "I know what I saw, and it sure wasn't one of those glimpses for a mere second out of the corner of my eye, but at great length as I approached him not once but twice. I also know that road like the back of my hand and it would be impossible to escape my sight that quickly. One moment he was walking and in a heartbeat he was gone. Just like that." Henry snapped his fingers to illustrate.

The feeling Henry got the instant he saw the strangely dressed man was similar to how I felt the night my husband and I saw a man on that same stretch of road. It was after midnight and we were driving home when suddenly we rounded the curve and a lanky man was standing almost in the center of the road. We slammed on the brakes and swerved to avoid hitting him, shocked that he didn't even attempt to move out of the way, in fact he didn't react at all. His head was slightly lowered and he looked straight ahead with sunken eyes, unmoving. We seemed more shaken than he appeared. My husband asked, "Did you see that?"

I was unsure if Ron was asking about the man or what he was wearing, which was a cowboy hat and a satiny robe over dark pants. Remember, I was unaware of Henry's encounter at this time I had never heard his story or had never heard of a similar sighting of a bizarrely dressed man walking on this road.

By this time my husband had stopped the car, so shaken we both were, but I didn't like the feeling the man's presence ignited, I asked, "What are you doing?"

My husband was already backing up, "What If something's wrong? Why would he be standing in the middle of the road like that?"

Mere seconds had passed from when we nearly hit the dazed man, yet when we backed up he was gone. Both of us exchanged bewildered looks. It was pitch black that night but our headlamps had illuminated him well, there was no mistaken what we saw. He had dark hair, strong bone features and appeared very dark under his eyes. In fact, having him suddenly appear in front of our car after we rounded the curve etched his image in both of our minds forever.

"You don't easily forget a strange looking character like that." Henry had mentioned, "Especially when it disappears before your eyes."

When Henry and I compared our stories it left us both speechless. But it was Henry who finally found his voice, after a ragged sigh he raked his hand across his balding head, "I'm glad I met you and we talked about this story, I always knew he had to be a ghost, but publicly admitting that takes a lot of courage. I must admit I am relieved that you saw him, too."

I asked Henry if he was aware of any suspicious or sudden deaths that had happened along this road, since he was a police officer and knew the proper measures to investigate unexpected deaths, "Of course I looked into it," Henry admitted, "it shook me up a lot so I spent a little time searching for murders or suicides that happened on the road and although I discovered that there had been a couple of deaths in the same area, they occurred inside someone's home, not on the road itself." Henry's face paled and he looked at me solemnly. "But there was one old fella who used to get picked up for public drunkenness and gambling long ago in an old store that had become a hang-out for some of the locals which wasn't too far from the area where we saw the oddly dressed figure. One of our officers was a rookie back then way before I was a grown man. He told me about it after I mentioned what had happened to me that full moon night. The officer recalled that most weekends he would cruise out there just to arrest him, believing he was saving the guy's life, because as he put it one night someone was going to run him over on that dark road with him walking home drunk all the time."

This revelation caught me by surprise. "So, did that man happen to die out there?" I asked.

Henry shrugged his shoulders, "No one knows. One day he just never came back, and no one knows what happened to him, his house sat empty for a year or so and life moved on."

I only paused for a moment, "So did you ask if that man ever wore a robe and cowboy boots and hat?"

Henry nodded that he had asked, "Yes, I did. And although he didn't wear a robe, he did favor the cowboy look. And sometimes when it rained he wore a poncho. Maybe what we thought was a silky robe was in fact a wet poncho...."

Like most ghost tales this one remains a mystery. But for Henry, my husband and I we believe the odd disturbance in Heiskell to be paranormal in origin.

Chapter 10

Night Patrol
(Gatlinburg, TN)

I didn't know what to think when I first saw the slow walking man, moving silently between the parked cars, his purpose obvious as he was dressed in uniform. He didn't make a sound his movements were fluid, yet his posture was rigid. I watched him for several moments, wondering if this prominent hotel in Gatlinburg, TN had a problem with vandalism or theft. In the past I rarely saw the security personnel in the hotels my family and I stayed at. Was this procedure supposed to make us feel safer to see him every hour on the hour walking the parking lot? Was it meant to deter potential vandals and thieves?

Inside the lobby and everywhere else on the grounds the hotel personnel was prompt and friendly, joyful most of the time, and the atmosphere promised relaxation and comfort. It wasn't a five star hotel, it wasn't considered first class, not quiet luxury, maybe back in the day it met that criteria, but in comparison to the newer establishments this hotel was a bit better than "nice enough", so why did the presence of a night watchman leave me feeling tense?

The second night as my family and I returned from our outings I scanned the parking lot in search of him but didn't see the tall man making his rounds. Admittedly I felt relief for his absence, rationalizing that maybe there had been a recent incident which had prompted a temporary need of frequent patrolling.

A couple of hours later when we left the premises for an unexpected jaunt to a local nearby convenience store for child friendly snacks I realized that my relief was short lived, this time I caught sight of him walking towards the parking lot from the breezeway between office and parking garage. The parking garage was small and always full, I hadn't considered the fact that he patrolled there as well. His presence and diligence to duty should have brought comfort instead of trepidation, but for whatever reason it simply caused restless stirrings inside of me.

On the third night I stood at the window and watched him for a while, a quiet man, determined as he walked with purpose between each row of vehicles, never cutting an aisle short, never showing distraction. After a few minutes I mentioned the guard to my husband, "I've never seen a guard anywhere we've stayed at before, maybe it's common at the ritzier hotels or I might expect them in crime ridden areas but is it really necessary here?"

"Maybe it's a sign of the times. I like the idea that our car is safe, and we are too." My husband responded.

He made a valid point and I knew it was logical, but in the back of my mind I sensed that something wasn't right. Maybe the average person wouldn't think twice about the night watchman, maybe it was protocol for this franchise or specific to this city, but we traveled frequently, at least five times out of the year we stayed in comparable hotels, I had never seen a guard except on the rare occasion we went all out, staying in fancier hotels with special amenities such as valet parking.

I kept watching for our watchman. And in hind sight I can't say that I saw him in the same location twice but I saw him distinctly. I witnessed other guests moving from their vehicles to the hotel or vice versa, I saw that he didn't verbally acknowledge anyone, and actually I don't think he gave a sideways glance to the guests.

When we were checking out at guest service the male clerk asked about our stay, I innocently inquired, "Do you have issues with stolen property or vandalism in the parking lot?"

The young man behind the desk conveyed a surprised expression, but remained upbeat in mannerism, "No, ma'am we rarely have issues of that nature. Did something happen during your stay?"

My husband chimed in, "No, our stay was perfect. We didn't have a single incident."

"Of course nothing happened," I reasoned, "You would have been notified immediately, but I have never seen a night watchman anywhere we've stayed until now."

The clerk's shoulder drew back and his brow lifted a bit, "Night watchman? Here?"

The uneasy stirrings returned. "Yes, I saw him every night of our stay."

Our clerk exchanged uneasy glances with the female clerk to his left as he shuffled our receipt to us, his head slowly rocking from side to side, "We don't have a night watchman. We have video surveillance which is monitored by hotel staff." I recognized the very moment when he visibly brushed us off, the very instant when his uneasiness eclipsed his joyful demeanor, when he wanted to end this conversation, "We're glad you enjoyed your stay and we hope you will stay with us again in the future."

My husband was eager to be on his way, but I lingered behind as my family walked away, both clerks tried to look as busy as possible which I distinguished immediately as them trying to appear occupied and unapproachable. I knew I was being a pest, and to be honest I didn't mind being too nosey, I stood there until finally the male clerk lifted his eyes and asked, "Is there anything else I can do for you?"

"Well, I was wondering why you aren't concerned that there is a man who patrols your parking lot and parking garage every night and is not an actual employee at this hotel."

The clerks again exchanged bewildered looks, "I haven't been informed that there is a patrolman. I am certain if I needed to know I would have been made aware." He gave a quick perfunctory smile then turned away from me. When someone deliberately blows me off I rarely drop the subject, maybe it's the stubbornness in me. I stood there as he feigned completing a task, and I knew it was all for show because the female clerk couldn't resist looking from me to him frequently.

I finally stepped closer to the desk, speaking in a polite, determined tone, "You see the reason it bothers me is that I need to know if this is a safe hotel, should I avoid staying here in the future?" I paused deliberately, then continued as calmly as possible, "We travel several times a year, and we love returning to hotels we like, but if something has happened here, maybe something bad that requires a security guard, I should have that information disclosed to me so that I can make an informed decision."

This brought his attention back to me, at first he turned and looked at me over his shoulder then he turned full bodied and faced me, "I have worked here for three years and we maintain an exemplary record, our hotel is very safe. I have worked days and nights and I haven't had an issue. If we had an issue it would be resolved immediately."

"That's why you have a security guard to handle any issues?" I prompted.

"We don't have a security guard, we have hotel staff who are trained to handle minor incidents, but we do *not* have an armed, uniformed officer. We are literally within close proximity to a police station. Other than noise disturbances and drunken guests or offensive guests we do not have the types of incidents to require an onsite security officer. Our maintenance personnel and management personnel makes the decisions of how to handle such infrequent incidents, and again we have extensive video surveillance which is monitored frequently by our staff. So please *do* feel safe here, and we invite and encourage you to stay with us in the future." He looked smug that he had handled the situation properly, and maybe he had diffused it to a small degree but I wasn't satisfied.

I looked to the female, who was very interested in our exchange, "I understand and I feel much safer, but why aren't either of you concerned that I have seen a man every night for one week patrolling the premises?"

It was a deer in headlight moment laden with a heavy silence.

I broke the quietness, "And if you have video surveillance maybe someone should review the footage this week. To pinpoint who is walking around after dark in uniform making this particular guest concerned about the vandalism or theft issues at this specific hotel. I am in a good frame of mind to speak to management." Though I doubted I would carry it that far.

The woman finally decided to speak, "That isn't necessary. *I* have worked here for five years and I know the history here, I assure you we do not have issues with theft or vandalism. In fact, I know we haven't employed a security guard since the 1970's." Her eyes averted to the male who had returned to his position in front of where I stood on the opposite side of the desk.

"I am relieved you disclosed that to me." I told her, "But again, when I have reported seeing a person imitating a security officer I can hope you feel a tiny twinge of concern, enough concern at least to check into it."

The woman leaned closer to me, "I can check into it, but it won't do any good, you see we can check the video surveillance every night this week from dusk to dawn and we won't see a night watchman on the video."

The male also leaned forward, "It's not that we don't believe you, we have heard this before, but we haven't seen him ourselves and most people don't. I am not trying to insult your intelligence, but the fact that you have seen him and you are adamant about it indicates you may be receptive to the next disclosure." The familiar exchange of uncertain glances between staff. He lowered his voice, "The reason we do not have a security guard here is because thirty one years ago, before this building was remodeled from a smaller, less impressive hotel, the security guard was murdered in the garage, savagely beaten to death."

The woman loomed closer, as if her proximity to me made the story more palatable, "Only the very sensitive or psychic guests have seen him, but the rumors circulate rampantly. I have heard about the night watchman who never stopped patrolling our premises, even though most of our building is new, and nothing much remains from the old establishment." Her pause is brief, "Sometimes people have said he walks through walls that weren't here when it was part of the bigger parking lot back then. But Dale and I, we haven't seen him. I guess we never will. We don't have the ability to see him." Their eyes were locked with mine and I sensed that they were holding their collective breaths hoping I wasn't offended.

I wasn't offended, I was at ease, I knew there was a reason I felt taken aback by the presence of the night patrolman, but at the time he had looked so real I couldn't have guessed it was an apparition, one of the most vivid I had ever seen. What was left to say at this point? I nodded my understanding and gratitude, placing a hand on the desk, a slight gesture, "Thank you for solving the mystery. You have a blessed day."

When I approached my family waiting patiently in the car my husband knew I was finally satisfied. "Everything ok now?" he asked.

"Yes. The mystery is solved; the hotel doesn't have an issue with vandalism or theft, in fact if they have any issues it is usually noisy guests or intoxicated guests." My eyes scanned the parking lot as we departed, I knew he wouldn't be there, the night patrolman, I had only seen him after dark.

"I didn't think there was a real threat." He dismissed the subject and began a conversation with the children.

Obviously there had been a threat or a danger thirty one years ago when the hotel was smaller and maybe more seedy, maybe it was just bad timing, or perhaps there was a personal conflict, but the horrible fact remained, the guard had been murdered. Obviously he had been a dedicated employee who took his position seriously even after death. "I will want to stay here again." I uttered and then allowed myself to get lost in the ensuing conversation with my family, finally at ease with the night patrol at the hotel we had stayed at.

The End

A Word from the Author:

Although the short stories for this book were written more than half a dozen years ago, many dramatic, unexpected and unsettling things happened to me and my family which disrupted the publishing of this book.

I hope you have enjoyed the stories contained herein.

I ask that if you will check out my other 2 books of short ghost stories. Also found on Amazon:

Ghost Tales & Superstitions of Southern Appalachian Mountains
Published in 2010

This is Tammy's first published book, sharing old tales from the deep Appalachian Mountains in the South, stories which were handed down for generations from her mouther to her and now to her readers.

Chasing Ghost Tales in Tennessee
Published in 2012

This is Tammy's second published book, which happened as a result of the author becoming a paranormal researcher to further expand her collection of ghost stories. These tales come from locations the author and her team of friends and paranormal enthusiasts visited and investigated, gathering enough phenomenon to declare that these locations are most likely **haunted.**

About the Author:

Tammy J. Poore lives in East Tennessee with her family and many pets.

She has always enjoyed a good ghost story and believes herself to have lived in an actual haunted house during her formative teenage years.

For almost a decade she was an avid paranormal investigator, which contributed to the stories published in her second book, (see previous page for details about her other books), which can also be found on Amazon.

For approximately 5 years she enjoyed much success with her own webpage and blog about paranormal experiences. These sites have since faded into oblivion, as her life faced a drastic upheaval and she lost access to the websites.

Tammy hopes to continue writing, and publishing stories in the future. If you are interested in more published material from Tammy, you can 'like' her Facebook page, search for "Ghost Tales and Superstitions from Southern Appalachian

Mountains" on Facebook. Drop a comment, or send a personal message, especially if you have some ghostly encounters which you would like to share with the author. She may never cease to Chase Ghost Tales in East Tennessee.

Tammy wishes to thank *YOU*, the reader, for buying this book, for taking the time to read this section to the end, ☺ and also for sharing her passion and love of simple ghost stories.

www.ingramcontent.com/pod-product-compliance
Lightning Source LLC
Chambersburg PA
CBHW030558130626
46552CB00006B/2593